My First

Disney
LiBRARY

Toys in Paradise • The Longest Day

Bath · New York · Singapore · Hong Kong · Cologne · Delhi
Melbourne · Amsterdam · Johannesburg · Auckland · Shenzhen

This edition published by Parragon in 2011
Parragon
Queen Street House
4 Queen Street
Bath BA1 1HE, UK

ISBN 978-1-4454-2412-5

Printed in China

Toys in Paradise

Andy ran around his room, throwing clothes into a bag. He would be leaving any minute. His best friend's family was going to Florida on holiday and had invited him to come along.

"You're going to have so much fun!" Andy's mother exclaimed as she helped him pack. "You'll go to the beach, and to amusement parks. I wish Molly and I could come along!"

After Andy and his mother left the room, Andy's toys came to life. They gathered on the floor beside Andy's bed.

"I'd give anything to go on a tropical vacation," said Bo Peep. "Just think of it. The sandy beaches, the blue ocean, the warm sunshine. And of course, the moonlit nights. It sounds so romantic." She smiled at Woody the cowboy doll.

"Not to me," Rex the dinosaur said. "There are sharks in the ocean. And what about sunburn?"

"Hey, I've got an idea," said Jessie the cowgirl. "Why don't we make our own tropical paradise, right here in Andy's room?"

"We wouldn't even have to fly," said Rex. He sighed in relief.

"I could use some down time," Slinky Dog admitted. "I've been feeling stretched to my limit lately."

"Yippee!" Jessie cried. "What do you think we'll need?"

"This might help," Woody suggested. The toys gathered around as he flipped open a pamphlet. "Andy's mum left this behind. This is where Andy is staying."

"Lounge chairs, umbrella, water," Buzz Lightyear the space ranger said. "We can find all this stuff right here."

Sarge and the Green Army Men went in search of a potted plant. Hamm and Rex raided the kitchen for Buster's water dish and some sponges. Bo found a doll's parasol in Molly's room.

Soon all of the supplies were gathered in the centre of the room.

"Next stop: Paradise!" Jessie exclaimed.

The toys got to work. In no time at all, they had created their own tropical paradise.

"Ahh, this is the life," Woody sighed. He and Buzz were stretched out on the lounge chairs they had made out of the shoebox tops and sponges.

"Wait a minute," Jessie said. "We forgot the sun."

"We can't forget the sun!" exclaimed Buzz. "Without the sun, our planet –"

"The pretend sun," Woody reminded him.

"Oh, right," Buzz replied. "I know just what we need." He dragged the desk lamp to the edge of the desk and turned it on. "Better put on some shades."

Rex and Hamm were standing beside the makeshift ocean.

Rex noticed Hamm looked a little sad.

"What's wrong?" Rex asked.

"What's an ocean without any waves?" Hamm said.

Woody and Buzz hopped off their lounge chairs. They each grabbed a side of the ocean and started tilting it up and down.

"Surf's up!" announced Woody.

Jessie enjoyed a lively game of volleyball with Bullseye. Afterwards, she sat by the water and admired the view. Then she realized that something was missing – an ocean breeze!

She got up and lassoed a knob on Andy's dresser. She tugged on the rope to make sure it was secure, then she began to climb.

When she made it to the top, she flipped a switch.

A slight breeze started on the floor below.

"What's that?" Woody said.

Within seconds, the wind picked up, blowing things everywhere.

The toys scurried for cover as the parasol and the beach chairs skittered across the room.

"Typhoon!" Rex cried, diving under the bed.

"It's OK!" Jessie called. She flipped off the switch and the wind stopped. "It was just the fan. I wanted to make our palm tree sway in the breeze. Is everyone okay?"

"Almost everyone," Woody said. He pointed towards the bed where Rex's tail poked out from under the bedspread.

It took a little while, but finally, Jessie and the rest of the toys convinced Rex t
come out of his hiding place.
He was still trembling with fear.

"I don't think I can survive
another relaxing vacation!" Rex said.

"Don't worry, Rex," Woody said.
"There won't be any more storms here
today."

"Woody's right," Jessie chimed in.
She put the parasol back in its place,
shading the lounge chairs from the
sun. "We're in for clear skies and warm
weather."

Rex walked back over to the
beach. "I hope Andy has a great trip," he said. "Because paradise can be fun . . . as
long as you're with good friends."

The Longest Day

"Could I have everyone's attention, please?" called Woody the cowboy doll. The toys in Andy's room quickly gathered around him.

"What is it?" Rex the dinosaur asked anxiously.

"Don't tell me there's another yard sale!" Wheezy the penguin exclaimed.

"Nope, it's good news!" Woody said. "Today is Andy's last day of school. Starting tomorrow, it's summer vacation! And you know what that means."

"We get to play with Andy and Molly all day, every day!" Jessie the cowgirl said. *"Yee-hah!"*

"I love summer," added Hamm the piggy bank. "Remember all the fun we had last year?"

"Sure do!" said Slinky Dog. "How about when Andy bounced Woody on the new trampoline!"

Woody laughed as he remembered bouncing over and over. "That sure was something," he said.

"My favourite part of last summer was when Andy set up a dinosaur jungle in the sandbox," said Rex.

"There's no doubt about it," said Woody. "Summers with Andy are the *best*."

"I want vacation to start *right now*," said Hamm impatiently.

"I know how you feel," said Woody, "but we've got a whole morning and afternoon to get through first. We'd better keep busy."

"How about playing Roundup?" cried Jessie. Bullseye the horse whinnied excitedly. He loved that game!

"Okay," said Woody. "Everybody grab something you can use as a lasso. Then try to round up as many objects as you can."

The toys scrambled to find something to use as a lasso. Rex found some dental floss, and Bo Peep found a broken rubber band. When everyone was ready, Woody called out, "Get set! Go!"

Rex had trouble with the floss. "My arms are too short to get any distance," he cried. "All I can lasso is myself!"

Bo Peep lassoed her sheep, and then Hamm.

Wheezy managed to lasso the Aliens and RC Car with his string. Jessie, meanwhile, was racing around on Bullseye, roping everything in sight!

CRASH! The lamp on Andy's nightstand came tumbling down. "Uh-oh," said Jessie, "I got a little carried away."

"We have to get this cleaned up before Andy gets home," Woody declared. "Could I have all the trucks over here, please?"

Woody attached some ropes to the trucks. "Take it away, fellas!" he called. The trucks slowly lifted the lamp back onto the nightstand. Then Woody climbed the fire truck's ladder and put the lamp shade back in place on top of the lightbulb.

"Sorry," Jessie said.

"Don't worry," said Woody. "Besides, now we're closer to Andy coming home."

"But it's still only morning," Rex protested. "This is the longest day of my life!"

"Don't despair, Rex," Buzz Lightyear the space ranger said. "There are plenty of other things we can do to take our minds off waiting."

"Like what?" asked Rex.

All eyes were on Buzz. "Hmmm," he said. He crossed his arms, accidentally pushing one of his buttons. A red light shot across the room. That gave Buzz a great idea. "What about a round of laser tag?" he asked.

"Okay," said Buzz. "Here are the rules: I chase after you, and if my laser hits you, you're out. Everybody got it?"

"You can't catch me," Slinky Dog taunted. He ran until the front half of his body was stretched clear across the room, but his back half was still standing right in front of Buzz.

"Tag!" shouted Buzz, beaming his light on Slinky Dog's tail. "You're out!"

"Aw, nuts," said Slinky Dog. "I'm just not built for this game."

"What's the matter, Buzz?" called Woody. He was riding on RC. "Are we too fast for you?" They zipped this way and that while Buzz tried to tag them.

"Woody, look out!" shouted Buzz.

"Trying to distract me, eh?" Woody replied. "Well, I'm not falling for that old trick." As soon as the words were out of his mouth, he and RC slammed into the rubbish bin and wiped out.

"Tag," said Buzz as he shined his beam on each of them.

After they'd cleaned up the mess from the bin, the toys decided to play hide-and-seek.

They took a vote to see who would be "it." They picked Hamm.

"One, two, three . . ." he counted as everyone hid. Woody and Wheezy scurried into the closet. Rex and Buzz ducked under the bed. Bo Peep and her sheep tucked themselves beneath a cardboard box. Soon, not a toy was left in sight.

The toys waited . . . and waited . . . and waited, but Hamm didn't come to look for them. Woody realized Hamm had stopped counting a long time ago. He stuck his head out of the closet and heard a low, snoring sound. Hamm was asleep!

"Hamm!" shouted Woody. "Wake up!"

"Oh, sorry," said Hamm, "I didn't get much sleep last night. tossed and turned, and every time I moved, my change made an awful racket."

"The important thing is, you're awake now," said Woody. "Now go find those toys."

"Ready or not, here I come!" Hamm called. He walked off to look for the toys.

He found Rex first. The dinosaur's tail had been easy to spot sticking out from nder the bedspread.

Finally, the only toys still hiding were Sarge and his men.

"Maybe they went on a mission," suggested Woody.

Hamm climbed up on the desk and stuck his head out of the   window. "Sarge!" he yelled, "are you there?"

"Negative!" cried Sarge, appearing on the drawbridge of a   castle made of building blocks. The rest of the Green Army Men began popping up on balconies and in tower windows.

"Wow! Neat castle!" said Rex.

"Andy built it last night," Woody explained.

"Say, could we play knights-and-dragon?" Rex asked hopefully.

"Hmmm," said Woody. "But who would play the dragon?"

"Me! I could do it!" volunteered Rex.

"And who would play the knights?" Woody said.

"Request permission for me and my men to play the knights defending the castle from the fire-breathing dragon!" shouted Sarge.

"Permission granted," Woody replied. "Let the battle begin!"

Rex pretended to attack the
castle again and again, letting out a
roar each time. Sarge and his men
were always able to push him
back over and over.

Then suddenly, Andy's puppy,
Buster, came skidding into the
room. When he saw the toys inside
the castle, he attacked it for real!

"Bad Buster!" Woody said as the dog ran out of the room. He hurried over
to the mess and helped the Green Army Men out from under the blocks.

"What are we going to do now?" said Rex looking at the mess.

"We're going to have to rebuild the castle so it looks exactly like it did
before," Woody replied.

The toys worked together restacking the blocks. When they were finally done, the castle looked as good as when Andy built it!

Woody looked over at the clock. "We've still got a little time before Andy gets home," he said. "What else can we do?"

"I need to spruce myself up," Bo said as she peered in the mirror. She fixed her bonnet, which had been sliding off her head.

"I'm tired!" Rex said. "Building a castle is hard work."

Woody agreed. The toys all took some time to rest so they'd be ready to play again when Andy got home.

By three o'clock, the toys were all waiting anxiously for Andy.

"What's taking him so long?" Hamm wondered aloud.

"I'm positive this is the last day of school," said Woody. "But let me check the calendar." Woody climbed up on the desk.

The rest of the toys waited on the floor, eager to hear what Woody would say. When Woody came back to the edge of the desk and looked down, the other toys knew the news wasn't good. "I'm sorry, guys," he said. "There's a note on the desk. It appears there's a party after school."

"So what time will Andy get here?" asked Rex.

"I don't know," said Woody. "Look, it's only a few more hours, and then we'll have the whole summer with Andy."

While the other toys drifted off to find something to do, Woody stretched out to sleep. The happy shouts of children filled his dreams. Suddenly, someone was shaking him awake.

"Woody!" cried Bo. "Wake up!"

Woody opened his eyes. He could still hear children's voices. He looked out the window and saw lots of kids in Andy's backyard. He wasn't dreaming, after all! Andy's entire class was here for the end-of-school party! No wonder it took him longer to get home, Woody thought.

Footsteps thundered up the stairs, and Andy and his classmates burst into the room.

"Wow! Great toys!" a boy shouted as he picked up Buzz and Rex. The other kids grabbed more toys until Woody and all his friends were part of the celebration.

This is going to be the best summer ever! Woody thought happily.

The End